Once upon a tin

10 classic fairy tales from different parts of the world , reimagined and illustrated .
A treat for children of all ages!

Table of contents

Preface

Join me on a spellbinding journey through this book, where you'll uncover reimagined classic tales from around the world, filled with delightful surprises. Born from my childhood love for fairy tales, this collection aims to captivate readers by introducing unexpected twists while preserving the essence of the original stories.

In this book, you'll encounter familiar characters in new situations, experience epic battles of good versus evil, and embark on thrilling quests where courage, wisdom, and kindness prevail. These stories, infused with magic and wonder, also teach valuable life lessons that inspire readers to embrace inner strength and remain true to themselves.

Drawing from diverse cultural sources, such as Aesop's fables and Arabian nights, these adapted tales celebrate both the similarities and differences among various folklore traditions. My hope is that these fresh narratives will not only entertain but also spark curiosity about the rich tapestry of global folklore and fairy tales.

As you delve into these reimagined stories, let your imagination take flight and perhaps be inspired to create your own magical tales. So, dear readers, find a cosy spot and embark on an unforgettable journey through enchanted realms.

Yours in wonder and magic,

Kallol H

The frog and the princess

Once upon a time, in a land far away, a beautiful and spirited princess named Amelia lived with her father, King Harold. She spent her days wandering through the kingdom's lush gardens and enchanted woods, delighting in the wonders of nature. But despite her worldly explorations, the princess had never experienced true love.

One day, while playing near a deep well, Princess Amelia accidentally dropped her prized possession, a golden pearl, into the murky depths. As she wept by the well, a mysterious frog surfaced from the water and spoke to her.

"Princess, why do you weep so bitterly?" the frog asked with genuine concern.

"Dear frog, I've lost my precious golden pearl, and I fear it is gone forever," replied Amelia, wiping away her tears.

"If I were to retrieve your pearl , would you grant me a favour in return?" the frog inquired.

Curious, Amelia asked, "What favour do you seek?"

The frog replied, "I long for companionship, and if you let me eat from your plate, drink from your cup, and sleep in your bed for three nights, I will fetch your golden pearl."

Amelia hesitated but finally agreed, thinking it a small price to pay for the return of her cherished possession. True to his word, the frog dove into the well and emerged with the golden pearl. Overjoyed, Amelia quickly ran back to the castle, forgetting her promise.

That evening, during dinner, the frog appeared at the castle door, seeking to claim his reward. The king, puzzled by the creature's presence, asked his daughter about the frog. Reluctantly, Amelia confessed her promise to the frog. King Harold, a man of integrity, urged his daughter to honour her word.

Over the course of the three days, Amelia begrudgingly shared her meals, her home, and her time with the frog. Their conversations were often filled with playful banter and unexpected wisdom.

On the first night, the frog spoke of his experiences in the enchanted woods, regaling Amelia with stories of magical creatures and hidden treasures. Amelia was captivated, realising she had only seen a fraction of her kingdom's wonders.

"Princess Amelia, you have so much to learn from this land. I can be your guide if you allow me," the frog offered.

Amelia hesitated but finally agreed, her curiosity piqued.

The following day, the frog took Amelia on a journey through the woods. They encountered a family of deer and Amelia, moved by their beauty and innocence, asked the frog if they could stay and watch the creatures.

"Of course, my princess. I want you to experience the magic of our kingdom," the frog replied, a gentle smile forming on his lips.

Over the next two days, the frog continued to share his knowledge and love for the kingdom with Amelia. He showed her a hidden grove where butterflies danced, and they listened to the melodic songs of the nightingales in a moonlit glade. Amelia found herself drawn to the frog's wisdom and passion for his home.

On the third and final night, as they sat by the fire in Amelia's bedroom, the frog asked, "Princess, do you think it's possible to see the beauty in all things, even when they are not as they seem?"

Amelia looked into the frog's eyes and replied, "I believe so. I've learned so much from you and have come to appreciate the hidden wonders of our kingdom."

The frog smiled warmly, touched by her words. As the night drew to a close, Amelia felt an unexpected affection for the frog, who had shown her a world she had never known. Overwhelmed by gratitude, she leaned in and kissed the frog on his cold, wet lips.

In that instant, a bright light enveloped the room, and before Amelia stood a tall, handsome prince. Astonished, she gasped, "Who are you, and what happened to the frog?"

The prince, smiling tenderly, replied, "I am Prince Alaric, cursed by a wicked witch to live as a frog until I receive true love's kiss. You, dear Amelia, have broken the spell with your kind heart and genuine affection."

Amelia, moved by the revelation, found herself falling deeper in love with Alaric, the prince who had once been her amphibious companion. They spent their days exploring the kingdom together, sharing their dreams and aspirations, and growing ever closer.

As Amelia and Alaric spent more time together, they began to notice a pattern to his transformations. Each night, when the moon was at its peak, Prince Alaric transformed back into a frog, only regaining his human form when kissed by the princess the following morning. This puzzled them both, so they decided to seek answers.

The couple ventured deep into the enchanted woods, searching for the wise old witch who had cursed Alaric. After many days of travel, they finally found her living in a small, secluded cottage. The witch, now old and weary, recognized Prince Alaric and welcomed them into her home.

"Ah, young prince," she said, "I see you've found your true love and broken the curse. But it seems there is still some lingering magic."

Alaric replied, "Indeed, wise one. Each night, I am still cursed to return to my frog form, only to regain my human appearance upon being kissed by my beloved Amelia. Please, tell us how to completely break this curse."

The witch stroked her chin thoughtfully and replied, "The spell was designed to teach you a lesson in humility and the importance of true love. The lingering magic is a reminder of that lesson. You see, Prince Alaric, true love is not only about loving someone for who they are but also accepting and cherishing their imperfections. For the curse to be entirely broken, you and Amelia must demonstrate your unwavering love and commitment to one another, no matter the form you take."

With this newfound knowledge, Amelia and Alaric returned to their kingdom, determined to prove their love and break the remaining curse. They held a grand ceremony, declaring their love and commitment to each other in front of the entire kingdom. Amelia vowed to love and cherish Alaric in both his human and frog forms, while Alaric promised to honour and protect Amelia with all his heart.

As the couple exchanged their vows, the witch, who had been secretly observing the ceremony, was deeply moved. She realised that Amelia and Alaric's love had grown beyond her expectations and that they had learned the lesson she had intended. Touched by their dedication, the witch decided to reward the couple by lifting the remaining curse.

As the ceremony concluded, the witch appeared before the couple and said, "Amelia and Alaric, your love has proven itself to be true and enduring. As a testament to your unwavering commitment, I shall remove the final remnants of the curse."

With a wave of her wand, the witch lifted the curse, ensuring that Prince Alaric would no longer transform into a frog at night. The kingdom rejoiced, and the couple continued to rule side by side, their love an example to all.

Red riding hood and the evil witch

Once upon a time in the small village of Rosedale, there lived a young girl named Rosaline, who was lovingly called Red Riding Hood by the villagers. She was known for the bright red cape she wore, a gift from her grandmother. The cape was beautifully woven with intricate patterns and was said to be magical, passed down through generations.

Red Riding Hood lived with her mother, a humble seamstress, on the edge of a vast and mysterious forest. Her mother often warned her to be careful when venturing into the woods, as it was home to strange creatures and enchanted beings.

One sunny morning, Red Riding Hood's mother received an urgent letter from her own mother, the grandmother. In the letter, she complained of a terrible illness that left her weak and bedridden. Red Riding Hood's mother immediately prepared a basket of homemade bread, jams, and other treats to help her mother recover. She then asked Red Riding Hood to deliver the basket to her grandmother's house, deep within the woods.

Before Red Riding Hood set off on her journey, her mother warned her, "Now, listen carefully, my dear. You must stay on the path and never speak to strangers. The woods are full of enchanted beings, and not all of them have good intentions."

Red Riding Hood nodded solemnly, taking the basket from her mother. As she entered the forest, she marveled at its beauty. Sunlight filtered through the leaves, casting dappled shadows on the ground, and a chorus of birds sang sweet melodies.

As she walked along the path, Red Riding Hood encountered an old, bent-over woman. The woman looked weak and frail, with a ragged shawl wrapped around her shoulders. Her eyes were cloudy and unfocused, and she appeared to be lost.

"Excuse me, dear," said the old woman, "I seem to have lost my way. Could you help me find the path back to my home?"

Remembering her mother's warning, Red Riding Hood hesitated but couldn't ignore the woman's pitiful state. "Of course," she replied, "but I must be quick. I am on an important errand to deliver a basket of food to my sick grandmother."

The old woman's eyes lit up with interest. "Your grandmother, you say? How sweet of you to care for her so."

They walked together for a while, and the old woman asked Red Riding Hood about her life in the village. Red Riding Hood, ever trusting, shared stories about her friends, her mother, and the magical red cape she wore.

As they chatted, Red Riding Hood noticed a large, dark figure lurking in the shadows. It was a wolf, with thick, grey fur and piercing yellow eyes. The wolf stepped forward and addressed Red Riding Hood.

"Good day, young lady. My name is Wulfric, and I am the guardian of this forest. I couldn't help but overhear your conversation with this old woman. I must warn you, not everyone is who they seem to be."

Red Riding Hood was startled but remembered her mother's words. "Thank you, Wulfric, but I must be on my way. I have a task to complete, and my mother warned me not to talk to strangers."

Wulfric bowed his head. "Very well, but remember my words. Be cautious, and do not trust too easily."

Red Riding Hood and the old woman continued on their way. As they approached a fork in the path, the old woman suddenly pointed to the left. "There is my home, dear. Thank you for your kindness. Before you go, could you fetch me a bouquet of flowers? They would cheer me up greatly."

Red Riding Hood hesitated but decided to help the old woman. She picked a few wildflowers from the side of the path, handed them to the old woman, and said, "Here you go. I hope these brighten your day."

The old woman thanked Red Riding Hood and hobbled away, disappearing into the woods. Red Riding Hood resumed her journey, following the path deeper into the forest.

Meanwhile, the old woman, who was none other than the evil Grandma in disguise, cackled wickedly. She had learned about Red Riding Hood's magical cape and wanted it for herself. She knew that the cape would give her immense power, which she planned to use for her sinister purposes.

As Red Riding Hood continued her journey, she came across a group of animals - a fox, a rabbit, and two birds - who appeared to be arguing. She approached them cautiously and asked, "What's the matter, my little friends?"

The squirrel, the most vocal of the three, said, "We've just heard that the forest is in grave danger. An evil enchantress has returned, and she seeks to take control of the entire forest using a magical cape. She has already deceived many creatures, causing chaos and mistrust among us."

Red Riding Hood gasped. "That's terrible! But how can I help?"

The birds spoke up, "We've heard that you possess a magical red cape. It is said that the enchantress is after it. You must protect the cape and keep it away from her clutches. We believe she has disguised herself as an old woman to deceive you."

Red Riding Hood thought about the old woman she had met earlier and felt a pang of fear. "What should I do?" she asked.

The rabbit, who had remained silent until now, finally spoke. "You must continue on your journey to your grandmother's house, but be vigilant. Trust your instincts and, most importantly, remember the words of the wise wolf you met."

With a newfound sense of determination, Red Riding Hood thanked the animals and continued on her way. Upon reaching her grandmother's house, she noticed the door was slightly ajar. She cautiously stepped inside, calling out softly, "Grandmother? It's me, Red Riding Hood. I've brought you some food to help you feel better."

Her grandmother's voice, weak and raspy, responded, "Come in, my dear. I'm in the bedroom, too weak to get up."

As Red Riding Hood entered the bedroom, she saw her grandmother lying in bed, covered in blankets. But something seemed off. Her grandmother's eyes were darker, and her hands appeared bony and twisted.

"Grandmother, what's wrong with your eyes and hands?" Red Riding Hood asked nervously.

The figure in the bed cackled, and in an instant, the illusion was shattered. There, in place of her grandmother, was the evil enchantress, the old woman Red Riding Hood had met earlier.

"I must thank you, dear," she sneered. "You've led me right to the very thing I desire - your magical cape."

As the enchantress lunged towards Red Riding Hood with a sinister grin, the young girl let out a desperate cry for help. In that heart-pounding moment, Wulfric, the wolf, burst through the window with a ferocious snarl, his powerful form blocking the enchantress's path.

"You shall not harm this girl or take her cape," Wulfric growled, his voice thunderous and filled with rage. "The forest has suffered enough under your wickedness."

Taken aback by the wolf's sudden appearance, the enchantress hissed venomously, gathering her dark magic to unleash a powerful spell. Wulfric leaped towards her, his sharp claws aiming for the evil witch. The two supernatural beings clashed with an intensity that shook the very foundations of the house. Their battle was a whirlwind of magical energy and raw power, as they fought fiercely, neither willing to yield.

Red Riding Hood watched in horror, her heart pounding in her chest, as the wolf and the enchantress exchanged ferocious blows. The room seemed to quiver with each strike, as if it could crumble to the ground at any moment. The enchantress, realizing that she was evenly matched with the fearsome wolf, let out a final, frustrated scream.

"You may have stopped me this time, but I will return, and I will have that cape," she hissed, her voice dripping with menace.

With a flash of dark magic, the enchantress disappeared, leaving Red Riding Hood and Wulfric alone in the room. Red Riding Hood, still shaking from the encounter, managed to speak, "Thank you, Wulfric. You saved my life."

Wulfric nodded. "You were brave, young one. But we must make sure the enchantress can never return to harm you or the forest."

"What should we do?" asked Red Riding Hood.

"We must find a way to break the enchantress's power and protect the magical cape," Wulfric explained. "I know of an ancient spell that can bind her dark magic, but we must gather some rare ingredients to perform it."

Together, Red Riding Hood and Wulfric embarked on a new journey. They sought out the help of the fox, the rabbit, and the bird, who agreed to assist them in finding the ingredients necessary for the spell. Their journey took them to the furthest corners of the forest, where they encountered various challenges and discovered the true value of friendship and trust.

During their travels, they collected the needed ingredients: the petals of the Moonlit Orchid, the tears of a gentle Willow, and the essence of a Starfire Gemstone. With all the components gathered, they returned to Red Riding Hood's grandmother's house to perform the spell.

Wulfric carefully mixed the ingredients, creating a shimmering potion. "Red Riding Hood," he said, "you must dip the edge of your cape into this potion. It will imbue the cape with a protective aura, preventing the enchantress from ever using it for evil."

Red Riding Hood did as Wulfric instructed. The moment her cape touched the potion, it glowed brightly, and she could feel the power surging within it. The cape's magic was now protected from falling into the wrong hands.

With the spell complete, Wulfric turned to Red Riding Hood. "We have done well, young one. The enchantress's power is now bound, and she cannot threaten the forest or its inhabitants again."

"What about my grandmother?" Red Riding Hood asked, her eyes filled with concern.

Wulfric smiled. "During our journey, I managed to locate your true grandmother. The enchantress had imprisoned her in an enchanted sleep. I have freed her, and she is now resting, waiting for you to return."

Overjoyed, Red Riding Hood hugged Wulfric tightly. "Thank you, Wulfric. You've not only saved my life but also my grandmother's. I will never forget your kindness."

From that day on, Red Riding Hood and Wulfric became the best of friends. Red Riding Hood continued to visit her grandmother regularly, always cautious and aware of the lessons she had learned. Wulfric, the guardian of the forest, remained a steadfast protector of its inhabitants, tough it didn't stop them from having a picnic now and then in the forest with her real grandmother!

Pride and friendship

Once upon a time, in a magical forest, there lived a variety of animals with unique talents and characteristics. Among them were two unlikely friends, the Tortoise and the Hare. They were known throughout the land as the best of friends, despite their differences in speed.

Their friendship, however, was often met with scepticism and ridicule from the other animals. The Cheetah, the Eagle, and the Fox would often laugh at the Tortoise for his slow pace, especially when compared to his fast friend, the Hare. They could not fathom why the Hare would choose to be friends with someone so different from him.

One day, the animals gathered at their favourite meeting place, the Old Oak Tree, where the Tortoise and the Hare were enjoying each other's company. The chatter among the animals grew louder, and the taunts aimed at the Tortoise intensified.

"Look at the Tortoise, so slow and clumsy!" the Cheetah sneered. "Why would the Hare even want to be friends with such a slowpoke?"

"Yeah!" chimed in the Eagle, perched high above. "I bet the Tortoise couldn't even keep up with the Hare if they raced!"

The Tortoise, feeling the pressure and tired of the constant mockery, turned to his friend the Hare and said, "Hare, I challenge you to a race. I want to prove to everyone that our friendship is not defined by our speed, but by the love and respect we have for each other."

The Hare hesitated, worried about what the race might do to their friendship, but he could see the determination in the Tortoise's eyes. He agreed to the challenge, saying, "Tortoise, if this is what you need to prove our friendship to the others, I will race you. "

A large crowd of animals gathered to witness the race between the Tortoise and the Hare. The course was set, and the finish line was marked by a beautiful waterfall. The animals placed their bets, with many of them believing the Hare would surely win. The wise Owl, however, remained neutral, knowing that the true outcome of the race was beyond their understanding.

As the race began, the Hare dashed forward with incredible speed, leaving the Tortoise far behind.

But the Hare's heart was heavy, for he did not want to hurt his friend's feelings by winning too easily. So, as he passed by the Squirrel's tree, he stopped to help the Squirrel gather some nuts that had fallen to the ground.

"Thank you, Hare!" said the Squirrel, surprised by his kindness. "You're such a good friend."

Meanwhile, the Tortoise plodded along, feeling the weight of the other animals' expectations on his shell. He knew he couldn't win the race, but he also knew he had to try his best for the sake of his friendship with the Hare.

As the race continued, the Hare came across the Beaver, who was struggling to move a large log to build his dam. Without hesitation, the Hare stopped to help, using his strong legs to push the log into place.

"Thank you, Hare!" said the Beaver, grateful for the assistance. "You have a big heart."

On the other side of the forest, the Tortoise was making slow but steady progress. He was beginning to feel the exhaustion setting in, but he refused to give up. The thought of his dear friend the Hare waiting for him at the finish line kept him going.

As the sun began to set, the Hare came across a group of baby birds who had fallen from their nest. Seeing their distress, the Hare decided to stop once again, carefully placing each bird back into its nest.

"Thank you, Hare!" chirped the grateful mother bird. "You are truly a kind soul."

By this time, the Tortoise had reached the halfway point of the race. He looked around, and discovered that the hare was taking a nap under a tree , visibly tired from the tasks he had done so far.

"This could be my chance!" tortoise thought for a second. He wanted to finish the race while the hare sleeps. Then another voice in his head said "My pride has put our friendship at risk, and for what? To prove a point to those who will never understand?"

The Tortoise decided to forfeit the race and sat beside his friend.

The hare woke up soon and said "Torty, I'm sorry. I should have never agreed to this race. Our friendship is more important than any competition."

The Tortoise looked up at his friend and smiled. "You're right, Hare. I challenged you to this race out of pride and a desire to prove something to others. But I've realized that our friendship is stronger than what others think. Let's forget about the race and rest here together."

The two friends lay down under the tree, side by side, and took a much-needed nap. As they slept, the other animals began to grow restless, wondering what had happened to the two racers. The wise Owl, who had been observing the entire race, decided to speak up.

"Listen, everyone," said the Owl. "The true purpose of this race was not to determine who is faster, but to show us all the power of friendship. The Hare stopped to help others, and the Tortoise realized that their bond is more important than any competition. Perhaps we can all learn something from their actions."

The animals fell silent, reflecting on the Owl's words. They realized that their taunts and jeers had driven the Tortoise and the Hare to challenge each other, but in the end, their friendship had only grown stronger.

From that day on, the magical forest became an even more harmonious place, where all the animals lived together as friends, appreciating each other's unique qualities and talents. The Tortoise and the Hare continued to be the best of friends forever!

Balance of life

Once upon a time, in a lush green meadow, there lived a grasshopper named Gavin and an ant named Archie. Gavin was a carefree soul, who loved to sing and dance. He spent his summer days hopping from leaf to leaf, playing his fiddle, and entertaining everyone with his joyful music. His fellow grasshoppers admired him and often joined him in his merry-making.

Archie, on the other hand, was a hardworking and diligent ant. He understood the importance of preparing for the future, and so he spent his days gathering food for the winter. Archie led a team of ants, and together they tirelessly collected grains, leaves, and seeds, storing them in their cosy little anthill. The ants admired Archie for his determination and sense of responsibility.

One day, as Gavin was hopping along, playing his fiddle, he came across Archie and his team of ants. They were busily collecting food and carrying it to their anthill. Gavin stopped playing and said, "Hello, Archie! What a beautiful day it is! Why don't you take a break and join me in a song and dance?"

Archie looked up from his work and replied, "Hello, Gavin. It is indeed a lovely day. But we ants must work now so that we have enough food stored for the winter. We cannot afford to waste our days singing and dancing like you grasshoppers."

Gavin chuckled and said, "Oh, Archie, you always worry too much! We have plenty of food in the meadow. Winter is still far away. Come on, take a break, and have some fun!"

Archie shook his head and said, "I appreciate your offer, Gavin, but I must decline. I have a responsibility to my fellow ants. We must prepare for the winter." With that, Archie returned to his work.

As summer turned to autumn, and then to winter, the meadow transformed. The once green grass turned brown, and the leaves on the trees fell to the ground. The cold winds blew, and the food became scarce. Gavin, having spent his days singing and dancing, had not prepared for the harsh winter. Hungry and cold, he went to Archie's anthill, hoping to find some help.

Archie, being the kind soul that he was, took pity on Gavin and shared his food with him. "Gavin, you must learn from this experience. We ants worked hard all summer to prepare for the winter, while you sang and danced. Next year, you must work with us and help gather food."

Gavin nodded, thankful for Archie's generosity. "Thank you, Archie. I promise I will work with you next summer and learn the importance of preparing for the future."

When the warmth of spring returned, Gavin and Archie started working together. Gavin, true to his word, helped the ants gather food. But as the days went by, Archie noticed something was amiss. The ants, who had once worked with determination and purpose, became restless and bored. They were not as efficient as they used to be, and their productivity started to decline.

Archie was puzzled. "Why has our work become so tedious? We used to work tirelessly all day, and now we can barely focus on our tasks." He shared his concerns with Gavin, who replied, "I think I know what's missing, Archie. Music! When I used to play my fiddle, it lifted everyone's spirits and made their work seem less tiresome. Perhaps we should incorporate music into our work routine."

Archie realised that Gavin was right. Gavin's music had brought joy to the entire community and that was the one thing they all secretly enjoyed.

And so, Gavin and Archie started to play music while they worked. The ants' spirits lifted, and their work became enjoyable again. They sang and danced as they collected food, and their productivity increased. Soon, they had gathered enough food to last them through the winter, and they celebrated their success with a grand feast, with Gavin playing his fiddle and everyone dancing joyfully.

They both realised that there is a time for work and a time for play. We must learn to balance both and find joy in everything we do. Hard work and preparation are essential for a secure future, but we must also remember to enjoy the present moment and find ways to make our work fun and enjoyable.

The triumph of tweety

Once upon a time in a lush, green kingdom, there lived a clever and resourceful bird named Tweety. Known for her beautiful, melodious song and quick wit, Tweety was beloved by all the creatures of the kingdom. The kingdom was ruled by a ruthless king named King Magnus, who was known for his cruel nature and obsession with capturing and eating birds, believing that their songs would bestow upon him magical powers.

One day, while Tweety the bird was singing atop a tree, her enchanting voice caught the attention of the king.

Magnus summoned his most cunning minister, Sir Roderick.
"Sir Roderick," the king said, "I have heard of a remarkable bird in our kingdom with a voice so beautiful that it must possess magical powers. I want you to find this bird, capture it, and bring it to me. I must have its voice for myself."

Sir Roderick, eager to please the king, set out to find Tweety. Upon locating her, he devised a plan to deceive her by pretending to be her friend. He approached where Tweety was singing and greeted her warmly.

"Hello, Tweety. Your lovely singing has made you quite famous. I am Sir Roderick, a humble servant of the king. His Majesty has heard of your incredible voice and wishes to invite you to the palace to perform for him."

Tweety, flattered by the invitation, replied, "Thank you, Sir Roderick. I would be honoured to sing for the king."

As they journeyed to the palace, Tweety and Sir Roderick engaged in conversation, with Tweety asking many questions about the kingdom and the king. Although she was excited about the opportunity to perform, she couldn't shake the feeling that something was amiss.

Upon arriving at the palace, Tweety was taken to a luxurious chamber where she was told to wait for the king. While waiting, she overheard a conversation between the king and his advisors.

"Once we have captured Tweety's voice, we will become unstoppable," the king declared. "Imagine the power I will hold with her magical voice at my command!"

Tweety's heart raced as she realised the king's true intentions. Determined to outsmart him and save herself, she devised an ingenious plan to escape.

When the king entered the chamber to meet Tweety, she greeted him with a curtsy. "Your Majesty, it is an honour to be invited to sing for you. I have always admired your wisdom and leadership."

The king, flattered by her words, replied, "Thank you, Tweety. Your voice is truly a gift, and I am eager to hear you sing."

As Tweety prepared to perform, she noticed a vase filled with oil in the corner of the room. She suddenly had an idea.

"Your Majesty," she said, "I have a request. To ensure that my voice is at its peak performance, may I use some of the oil in that vase to lubricate my throat?"

The king, eager to hear Tweety's magical voice, agreed. "Of course, Tweety. Do whatever you need to prepare."

Tweety dipped her beak into the vase, pretending to drink some of the oil. Then, she subtly spilled some of it on the floor, creating a slippery puddle near the king and his advisors.

As she began to sing, the king and his advisors were captivated by her enchanting voice. They leaned in closer, wanting to absorb every note. Sensing the perfect opportunity, Tweety suddenly stopped singing and darted towards the window.

The king and his advisors, caught off guard, lunged for Tweety, but instead, slipped on the oil puddle she had created. As they struggled to regain their footing, Tweety flew out the window, narrowly escaping their grasp.

"Stop her!" the king shouted, but his advisors were too disoriented to act quickly enough.

Tweety soared through the sky, her heart pounding with both fear and exhilaration. She knew that she had outsmarted the king and his advisors, but her fellow birds were still in danger. Determined to protect them, she decided to concoct another plan.

As Tweety returned to her forest home, she gathered her bird friends and shared her harrowing experience at the palace. She revealed the king's sinister intentions and urged her friends to join her in a plan to ensure their safety.

"We must teach the king a lesson and make him realise that he cannot take advantage of our gifts for his selfish desires," Tweety said. Her friends, inspired by her courage and determination, agreed to help her.

Together, the birds devised a plan to create chaos in the kingdom.
The following day, as the sun began to set, Tweety and her friends executed their plan. They flew over the palace, their voices blending into an overwhelming cacophony. The king and his advisors, irritated by the noise, rushed outside to see what was happening.

As they emerged from the palace, the birds launched their assault, pelting the king and his advisors with fruits, nuts, and branches. The king and his advisors, overwhelmed and disoriented, retreated back into the palace, seeking shelter from the relentless barrage.

Realising that he had been defeated by Tweety and her friends, the king's arrogance and greed began to dissipate. He understood that he had underestimated the power of the birds' intelligence and unity and vowed never to pursue them again.

Tweety and her friends rejoiced, knowing that their courageous efforts had saved not only themselves but also the other birds in the kingdom. The tale of Tweety's triumph over the cunning king spread far and wide, serving as a reminder of the power of intelligence, ingenuity, and unity in overcoming adversity.

Wings of destiny

Once upon a time in the ancient land of Greece, on the magical island of Crete, there lived a brilliant inventor and craftsman named Daedalus. He was well-known for his amazing creations, and his reputation spread far and wide. One day, he was summoned by the powerful King Minos to design an intricate labyrinth to imprison a terrifying beast known as the Minotaur.

Daedalus, along with his young and curious son Icarus, worked tirelessly to create the labyrinth. It was a mesmerising masterpiece, filled with twists and turns, so confusing that even the cleverest of men could not find their way out. The Minotaur was trapped there forever.

However, fearing that Daedalus might reveal the secret of the labyrinth to others, King Minos decided to imprison Daedalus and Icarus within a tower in Crete.

As days turned into weeks, and weeks into months, Daedalus grew increasingly desperate to escape the tower and Crete. One day, while they sat in a dimly lit corner of the tower, Icarus asked his father, "Father, will we ever be free from this place? I miss the warm sun and the cool breeze."

Daedalus, his face etched with determination, replied, "Fear not, my son. I have a plan. We will escape, and we will fly like the birds in the sky. I promise."

Over the next few weeks, Daedalus collected feathers shed by the birds that flew overhead. He used these feathers and the wax from candles to fashion two magnificent pairs of wings—one for himself and one for Icarus. As he worked, he would often catch Icarus staring longingly at the wings, his eyes filled with wonder and excitement.

Finally, the day arrived when the wings were ready. Daedalus called Icarus to his side and said, "Today, my dear son, we shall break free from this prison and fly to our freedom. But you must listen carefully to my words, for if you do not heed my warning, our plan may end in tragedy."

Icarus nodded eagerly, his eyes shining with anticipation. "I promise, Father, I will listen to you."

Daedalus, his voice firm yet gentle, explained, "When we take flight, you must not fly too low, for the sea's dampness will make the wings heavy and cause us to fall. You must also not fly too high, for the sun's heat will melt the wax holding the wings together, and we shall plunge to our doom."

"I understand, Father," Icarus replied, his voice trembling with excitement. "I will follow your guidance, and we will soar to our freedom together."

With their wings securely fastened, Daedalus and Icarus took a deep breath and leaped from the labyrinth's highest point. The wind caught their wings, and they began to fly. The joy and exhilaration of soaring through the sky filled their hearts, and they reveled in their newfound freedom.

As they flew over the vast ocean, Icarus couldn't contain his excitement. "Father, this is amazing! We're truly free!" he shouted, his voice carried away by the wind.

"Yes, my son," Daedalus replied, smiling warmly. "But remember my words and stay close to me. Do not let the thrill of flight cloud your judgement."

For a while, Icarus obeyed his father's instructions and flew close by his side. But as they continued their journey, he became more confident and began to soar higher and higher, captivated by the beauty of the sky and the freedom it offered.

Daedalus, sensing his son's growing boldness, called out to him, "Icarus, my son,

heed my warning! Do not fly too high, for the sun's heat will be our undoing. Stay close to me and we shall reach our destination safely."

But Icarus, entranced by the euphoria of flight, could not hear his father's words. He continued to climb higher, marvelling at the world below him. The sun's warmth felt like a gentle caress, and he felt invincible.

Daedalus, his heart filled with dread, cried out again, "Icarus, please! You must listen to me! The sun's heat is dangerous. Descend, my son, before it is too late!"

Just as Daedalus' words reached Icarus' ears, he began to notice the wax on his wings softening. Panic filled his heart as he realised the gravity of his mistake. Desperate to save himself, he tried to descend, but the wax had already melted too much, causing feathers to fall off one by one.

"I'm sorry, Father!" Icarus cried out, his voice filled with fear and regret. "Please help me!"

Daedalus, his heart aching for his son, knew that he had to act quickly to save Icarus from certain doom. He swooped down, flying as fast as his wings could carry him, and caught Icarus just as the last of his feathers fell away.

Together, they plunged into the sea, but Daedalus, with his wings still intact, managed to keep them both afloat. As they clung to each other in the water, a gentle whale swam by, curious about the strange beings in its domain.

Icarus, still trembling from his near-death experience, nodded, and together they pleaded with the whale for assistance. Moved by their plight, the gentle whale agreed and carried them to the safety of the shore.

As they stood on the beach, soaked and exhausted but alive, Daedalus turned to Icarus, his eyes filled with relief and love. "My son, I am so grateful that we are both alive. But you must remember that listening to wise counsel is essential for our well-being. Disobeying my warning could have cost us our lives."
Icarus, tears welling up in his eyes, embraced his father tightly. "I am sorry, Father. I let the thrill of freedom cloud my judgement. I promise to heed your advice from now on."

The fisherman and the Jinn

Once upon a time, in a quaint little fishing village by the sea, there lived a fisherman named Omar. Every day, before the first light of dawn, Omar would set out on his rickety wooden boat, casting his net into the gentle waves, hoping for a good catch to feed his family and make a modest living.

One fateful day, as the sun rose and cast its golden rays upon the shimmering sea, Omar cast his net into the water, hoping for a bountiful haul. As he pulled the net back to the boat, he noticed it was heavier than usual. Excited, he thought, "Perhaps today is my lucky day! My net must be filled with fish!"

But to his surprise, when Omar finally managed to pull the net into his boat, there were no fish. Instead, he found an old, tarnished brass jar, sealed with a lead cap bearing strange symbols. Intrigued by this peculiar object, he thought to himself, "Maybe there is something valuable hidden inside the jar. Perhaps my luck hasn't run out after all."

With great effort, Omar pried the cap off the jar, releasing a thick, billowing cloud of smoke that filled the air. The smoke swirled and twisted, gradually taking the form of a towering Jinni, with fiery eyes and a fearsome expression.

Trembling with fear, Omar stared at the Jinni, who spoke in a deep, thundering voice, "At last, I am free! I am Zaraq, the Jinni of the bottle! For centuries, I have been trapped in that wretched prison by the great King Solomon himself. I am grateful for your help, fisherman. As a reward, I shall grant you three wishes. Choose wisely, for my power is vast."

Omar, though cautious, believed that Zaraq would keep his promise. He thought carefully about his wishes and said, "First, I wish for enough food to feed my family and ensure that they never go hungry again."

Zaraq waved his hand, and a feast of delicious food appeared before Omar. Overjoyed, Omar brought the food back to his village, where his family and neighbours feasted for days. However, as time passed, the villagers grew complacent, relying solely on Omar's endless supply of food. They stopped farming and fishing, causing the once-thriving village to become increasingly dependent on Omar's enchanted food. The overabundance of food soon led to wastefulness, and the villagers' health declined as they gorged on the rich fare.

For his second wish, Omar asked, "I wish for my humble boat to be transformed into a strong and sturdy vessel, capable of withstanding the fiercest storms and providing for my livelihood."

Once again, Zaraq waved his hand, and Omar's rickety boat transformed into a magnificent ship, its sails billowing in the wind and its hull gleaming in the sunlight. With his new boat, Omar set sail, catching more fish than ever before. However, the other fishermen in the village could not compete with Omar's newfound success. Their boats remained empty, and many of them were forced to abandon their trade. With the loss of their livelihoods, the fishermen and their families fell into poverty and despair.

Lastly, Omar made his final wish: "I wish for the power to heal any sickness, so that I may ease the suffering of those around me."

Zaraq granted his wish, and Omar found himself imbued with incredible healing abilities. Word of his miraculous power spread quickly, and soon, people from neighbouring villages flocked to him, seeking cures for their ailments. However, Omar's gift turned out to be a double-edged sword. As more and more people sought his help, he found himself overwhelmed by the endless stream of the sick and injured. He could not keep up with the demand, and his own health began to suffer from the constant strain.

Furthermore, the village's doctors and healers, who had once been respected members of the community, found themselves out of work as everyone turned to Omar for help. Many of these skilled professionals left the village, taking their knowledge and expertise with them. The village's healthcare system collapsed, leaving the inhabitants more vulnerable than ever before.

As the months passed, Omar realised the grim truth: Zaraq was an evil Jinni, and the wishes he had granted were actually curses in disguise. The village, once thriving and united, had become fractured and despondent. The people relied on Omar's enchanted food and healing abilities, but their reliance on his supernatural gifts had only led to further suffering and strife.

Desperate to break the curse, Omar sought the counsel of a wise old sage who lived on the outskirts of the village. The sage listened to Omar's tale and told him, "You must return to the spot where you first released Zaraq and summon him once more. Only then can you undo the damage that has been done."

With a heavy heart, Omar sailed back to the spot where he had found the brass jar. He called upon Zaraq, who appeared with a sinister grin, knowing full well the destruction his wishes had caused.

"Ah, fisherman, you have returned," said Zaraq. "Do you wish to make another bargain?"

"No," replied Omar firmly. "I have come to demand that you undo the wishes you granted me. You promised me good fortune, but you have only brought misery to my village."

Zaraq laughed wickedly. "Very well, fisherman. I shall undo the wishes, but only if you can answer this riddle: 'What can be broken without being held, and can bind the strongest of men?'"

Omar pondered the riddle, and with a flash of insight, he replied, "A promise can be broken without being held, and it can bind the strongest of men."

Zaraq's eyes narrowed, and with a wave of his hand, he undid the wishes he had granted. The enchanted food vanished, Omar's boat returned to its original state, and his healing powers disappeared. The village, free from the Jinni's curses, began to rebuild, rediscovering the value of hard work and self-reliance.

Omar returned to his humble life as a fisherman, grateful for the lessons he had learned from his encounter with Zaraq. He shared his story far and wide, teaching others about the dangers of seeking shortcuts to riches and success. And from that day forward, the village thrived once more, its people wiser and more resilient than ever before.

A golden lesson

Once upon a time, in a small village nestled amidst lush green fields and towering trees, lived a humble farmer named Jack and his kind-hearted wife, Emma. Life was simple, and they were content with their small piece of land, where they grew vegetables and raised a few farm animals. Among these animals was a plain-looking goose, named Gilda, which they had adopted a few years ago.

One morning, as they went about their daily chores, Jack and Emma were astonished to find a glittering golden egg in Gilda's nest. They could hardly believe their eyes! Excitedly, they took the egg to the village goldsmith, who confirmed that it was indeed made of pure gold. Jack and Emma rejoiced, knowing that their fortunes had taken a miraculous turn.

As days turned into weeks, Gilda continued to lay a golden egg every morning. Jack and Emma sold the eggs in the market, and their wealth grew steadily. Soon, they were able to renovate their small cottage into a grand mansion, wear fine clothes, and dine on lavish feasts. However, as their wealth increased, so did their greed.

One evening, while they were counting their gold coins, Emma said to Jack, "We are becoming richer by the day, but I can't help thinking about all the gold that must be inside Gilda. Imagine how much wealthier we could be if we had it all at once!"

Jack, stroking his chin, replied, "You're right, Emma. If we could get our hands on all the gold inside Gilda, we wouldn't have to wait for her to lay an egg every day. We would be the richest people in the entire village, maybe even the kingdom!"

Unbeknownst to them, Gilda was listening to their conversation from her nest. She was saddened by their greed and decided to teach them a lesson they would never forget.

The following morning, Jack and Emma eagerly went to Gilda's nest, expecting to find another golden egg. Instead, they discovered an ordinary, white egg. They stared at it in disbelief.

"What's going on, Gilda?" Jack asked, frowning. "Why have you laid a regular egg?"

Gilda just gazed at them, her eyes filled with wisdom but revealing no answers. Jack and Emma were baffled, but they chose to wait and see what would happen the next day.

To their dismay, Gilda continued to lay ordinary eggs for several days. As their once-abundant supply of gold began to dwindle, the couple started to realise the error of their ways. They missed the simple life they had once led and the happiness that came with it. Their newfound wealth had brought them nothing but worry and greed.

One evening, as they sat by the fireplace, Emma looked at Jack with tear-filled eyes and said, "I wish we had never found those golden eggs, Jack. Our lives were so much better before."

Jack sighed, nodding in agreement. "You're right, Emma. I miss our simple life, too. We took Gilda's gifts for granted and allowed greed to consume us. If only we could go back to the way things were."

Gilda, who had been silently listening from her corner, decided that the time had come for her to intervene. She waddled up to the couple and said, "Jack, Emma, I have heard your words, and I know that you are truly sorry for your actions. You have learned the importance of appreciating what you have and not letting greed take over your hearts."

Jack and Emma stared at Gilda in amazement, having never heard her speak before.

"Gilda! You can talk?" Emma exclaimed, her eyes wide with shock.

"Yes, Emma," Gilda replied, her voice gentle and soothing. "I have been blessed with the gift of speech and wisdom. I wanted to teach you both a valuable lesson about gratitude, patience, and the perils of greed."

Jack and Emma, filled with remorse, fell to their knees. "We are so sorry, Gilda," Jack cried. "We promise to never take your gifts for granted again and to share our good fortune with those in need."

Gilda nodded, satisfied with their heartfelt apologies and genuine transformation. "Very well, I will once again lay golden eggs for you, but remember to always value the simple joys of life, and use your wealth to spread kindness and generosity."

Jack and Emma thanked Gilda profusely, and from that day on, they were true to their word. Gilda resumed laying golden eggs, and the couple used their wealth to improve the lives of the villagers. They built a school, a hospital, and helped struggling families to get back on their feet. They also made sure to treat Gilda with love, care, and respect.

As the years passed, Jack and Emma grew old, content with the life they had built together. They were beloved by the entire village for their kindness and generosity, and their once-simple home had become a haven for those seeking help and support.

The wise and gracious Gilda continued to lay golden eggs, but now she did so not just for Jack and Emma, but also for the benefit of the entire village. Her magical gift had become a symbol of hope and prosperity, and her lessons on gratitude, patience, and the importance of valuing what one has were passed down through generations.

The Miracle with Govardhan Hill

Once upon a time in ancient India, the enchanting village of Vrindavan flourished under the loving care of its inhabitants. The village was home to Lord Krishna, believed to be an avatar of Lord Vishnu, the divine deity. The people of Vrindavan adored the divine child, and his extraordinary powers brought joy and wonder to their lives.

The villagers relied on agriculture for their livelihood, and rain was essential for the prosperity of their crops. Thus, they performed an annual ritual, the Indra worship or 'Puja', to please Lord Indra, the god of rain and storms, seeking his blessings for timely rainfall.

One year, as the villagers prepared for the Indra Puja, Krishna observed their blind devotion to the powerful deity. He believed that it was time to teach them a valuable lesson about the importance of respecting nature and its resources. So, Krishna approached his father, Nanda, and the village elders with a proposal.

"Father, why do we perform the Indra Puja every year?" Krishna asked innocently.

Nanda replied, "My son, we worship Lord Indra to ensure that he blesses us with rain, which is crucial for our crops and our very survival."

Krishna, with a gentle smile, said, "But Father, it is Mount Govardhan that provides us with fertile soil, water, and shelter. Shouldn't we honour the mountain instead of Lord Indra?"

Nanda and the village elders exchanged puzzled glances, but they couldn't ignore the wisdom in Krishna's words. So, they agreed to Krishna's suggestion and decided to worship Mount Govardhan that year.

The news of the villagers' decision spread like wildfire. When Lord Indra heard that the people of Vrindavan had abandoned their ritual to honour him, he was filled with rage. He vowed to punish the villagers for their insolence and teach them a lesson they would never forget.

As the villagers gathered to pay their respects to Mount Govardhan, dark clouds began to form in the sky above Vrindavan. Fierce winds started to blow, and a torrential downpour followed, threatening to drown the village and its inhabitants.

The terrified villagers turned to Krishna for help. "Krishna," cried one of the elders, "we followed your advice, and now Lord Indra is punishing us! What shall we do?"

Fear not," Krishna replied calmly, "I will protect you all." With that, he approached Mount Govardhan and, using his divine strength, lifted the entire hill with his little finger. "Come, my friends, take shelter under the mountain with your families and cattle," he said.

The villagers were amazed by Krishna's miraculous feat, and they quickly took refuge beneath Mount Govardhan. For seven days and nights, the storm raged on, with relentless rain and howling winds. But under Krishna's protection, the villagers remained safe and dry.

Up in the heavens, Lord Indra watched in astonishment as his most powerful storm failed to break the spirit of Vrindavan's people. He finally understood that he was dealing with no ordinary child, but an incarnation of Lord Vishnu himself.

Humbled, Lord Indra ceased the storm and descended to Vrindavan to beg for Krishna's forgiveness. "Forgive me, Lord Krishna," he implored, "I was blinded by pride and arrogance. I have learned the importance of humility and compassion, and I promise to be a better guardian to your people."

Krishna smiled and said, "Lord Indra, remember that the love and devotion of the people are earned through kindness and understanding, not through fear and punishment. Let this be a lesson for us all."

With a grateful nod, Lord Indra returned to his heavenly abode, a changed deity, committed to his newfound wisdom and the lessons he had learned from Krishna.

Having witnessed the extraordinary events, the people of Vrindavan came out from under Mount Govardhan. They thanked Krishna for his divine intervention and protection, their hearts brimming with gratitude.

"My friends," Krishna said to the villagers, "let this be a reminder to us all that it is essential to respect and cherish the bounties that nature provides. We must not place our faith in one entity alone, but rather understand the interconnectedness of all creation."

The villagers nodded in agreement, their eyes filled with admiration and love for the divine child who had saved them from disaster. They vowed to honour and preserve the natural resources that sustained their village and to treat each other, as well as the world around them, with respect and kindness.

Adventure of three pigs

Once upon a time, in a beautiful and lush green valley, there lived three sibling pigs. Each had a unique personality, but they all shared a common desire: to build their own homes and live independently. The pigs knew that their valley was also inhabited by a cunning and ravenous wolf, so they understood the importance of building strong, secure houses.

The youngest pig, Penny, was known for her laziness and carefree attitude. She believed in enjoying life to the fullest and never really worried about the future. One sunny day, she decided to build her house from straw. Gathering the materials was quick and easy, and she spent the rest of her day relaxing.

Penny's older brother, Peter, was slightly more industrious but still lacked foresight. He preferred spending his time playing and exploring the valley with his friends. When the time came for him to build his house, he chose sticks as his material. Constructing the house took a bit longer than Penny's, but soon enough, he had a cosy stick abode and plenty of time left for fun.

The eldest of the three pigs, Paul, was the most diligent and thoughtful. He understood the importance of building a strong and secure home to protect himself from the dangerous wolf. He spent days collecting and preparing bricks, meticulously constructing his house with great care and precision. As he worked tirelessly, his younger siblings would often tease him.

"Paul, you're working too hard! Come have some fun with us!" Penny would call out, giggling as she lounged in the sun. "Yeah, lighten up! We built our houses in no time, and now we're enjoying our freedom!" Peter chimed in, tossing a stick for his pet squirrel.

But Paul would just shake his head and reply, "I'm building a strong house that will protect me from the wolf. You two should be more careful."

A few days after the completion of their homes, the cunning and hungry wolf arrived in the valley. He had heard whispers of the three little pigs and their new homes and saw them as an opportunity for an easy meal.

The wolf approached Penny's house of straw first. He could hardly believe his luck. Licking his lips, he called out, "Little pig, little pig, let me in!"

Penny, frightened by the sudden appearance of the wolf, quickly replied, "Not by the hair of my chinny chin chin!"

With a wicked grin, the wolf responded, "Then I'll huff, and I'll puff, and I'll blow your house down!" True to his word, he inhaled deeply and blew out a mighty gust of wind. The straw house collapsed, and Penny ran towards Peter's house and took shelter there.

Feeling frustrated, the wolf moved on to Peter's house of sticks. He approached the house and shouted, "Little pigs, little pigs, let me in!"

Trembling, Peter answered, "Not by the hair of my chinny chin chin!"

The wolf laughed, "Then I'll huff, and I'll puff, and I'll blow your house down!" Once again, he huffed and puffed, and the house of sticks came crashing down. Peter & penny both bolted towards Paul's house and took shelter there.

By now, the wolf's appetite was insatiable. He approached Paul's house of bricks, confident that he could bring it down just as easily as the others. "Little pig, little pig, let me in!" the wolf demanded.

Paul, standing strong and unafraid, replied, "Not by the hair of my chinny chin chin!"

"I'll huff, and I'll puff, and I'll blow your house down!" the wolf roared, fully expecting the brick house to crumble like the others. He huffed and puffed with all his might, but the brick house stood strong, not even a single brick out of place.

Frustrated and angry, the wolf shouted, "You may have built a strong house, but I'll still find a way in and eat you up!"

Paul, unfazed, responded, "You won't succeed, Mr. Wolf. I've built this house with hard work and determination, and it will protect me from your wicked ways."

The wolf, realising that huffing and puffing wouldn't work, devised a new plan. "I'll climb down the chimney and catch that pig off guard," he thought to himself, smirking at his own cleverness.

Meanwhile, inside the house, Paul anticipated the wolf's next move. He quickly placed a large pot of water on the fireplace and started a roaring fire beneath it.

The wolf climbed onto the roof and squeezed into the chimney, eager to catch pigs by surprise. But as he slid down the chimney, he was met with an unpleasant surprise of his own. He landed straight into the boiling pot of water with a loud splash.

The wolf yelped in pain and fled the house, never to bother the pigs again. Paul, having outsmarted the wolf and saved his own life through hard work and perseverance, became a hero in the valley.

From that day on, the other animals in the valley learned the importance of diligence, planning, and dedication in overcoming adversity and danger. Paul's courage and wisdom became an example for all, and his story was passed down through generations.

The end!

Printed in Great Britain
by Amazon

21477439R00033